WARNING

This book contains sexually explicit scenes and adult language. It may be considered offensive to some readers. This book is for sale to adults ONLY.

* * * * * * * * * * * * * * * * *

Please store your files wisely where they cannot be accessed by underage readers.

Please feel free to send me an email. Just know that these emails are filtered by my publisher. Good news is always welcome.

Dexter Chase - **dexter_chase@awesomeauthors.org**

About the Publisher

4Fun Publishing, a member of **BLVNP Incorporated**, 340 S. Lemon #6200, Walnut CA 91789, info@blvnp.com / legal@blvnp.com
NOTE: Due to the highly emotional reaction of some people to works of erotic fiction, any email sent to the above address that contains foul language or religious references is automatically deleted by our anti-spam software and will not be seen. All other communications are welcome.

DISCLAIMER

Gay Romance Erotica

MASTERED

SENSUAL TALES FROM ANCIENT EGYPT

DEXTER CHASE

Mastered

Sensual Tales from Ancient Egypt

Gay Romance Erotica

By: Dexter Chase

© Dexter Chase 2014

ISBN: 978-1-68030-046-8

Chapter 1

The Egyptians were rampant, raiding across the middle sea, raping and pillaging, but worst of all taking many slaves.It was always the youngest and most nubile of females and the prepubescent and middle teen boys. Those chosen were taken as sex slaves, to be used for their masters own sexual satisfaction and at times to be shared by other masters and forced to take part in orgies. The orgies that would make the later Roman ones pale into insignificance.

I knew about the Roman orgies because that Empire grew as I too grew up, and I would eventually be taken there as an overseer for all the younger slaves that were taken from Egypt. Slaves in Egypt were invariably naked and most of the large houses had a bevy of young male and female slaves kept almost entirely for sex.

It was into one of these great houses that I was taken after being captured in one of the raids. I, too became one of those slaves all those years ago. I had passed into puberty and grown into a quite imposing youth at eighteen at the time I was captured. My new master was probably no older than thirty five but already he had a son my own age and several younger ones. He was a high ranking soldier and as one would expect he had a magnificent body. Before I became a slave, I had been mentored by a friend of my father's after puberty so I was well practiced in the art of man to man sex, us Greeks were not at all conscious that men having sex with boys was anything abnormal.

The Egyptians didn't think like that so I was quite surprised that my master would fuck me frequently but I noticed he never allowed other men to fuck his eldest son. The eldest son was called Ptolemy, at eighteen he was almost too pretty to be a boy, made more so by the makeup he used on his eyes. I think I started to fall in love with him from the first day I saw him. He was always beautifully dressed and wandered around the villa with seemingly nothing to do. He would watch me work sometimes when his father was away and as I started to learn his language, he started talking to me.

By the time I was twenty his father had rather lost interest in me so I was trained to look after Ptolomy, his clothes all had to be perfect and ready to use at any time. The first time I left some of his clothes out instead of carefully putting them away I found that he was very strong and could be quite wicked.

"Ajax, how dare you leave my clothes like this?"

I realised he was very angry and fell to my knees begging his forgiveness.

"Of course I'm going to forgive you, after I have punished you. Come."

I knew where we were going. I had been to the punishment room before whenever I had displeased my master. I resigned myself to receiving a huge tranche of pain as I was whipped and knew that I would probably be in bed for a week unable to recline on my back. I was surprised at what happened, it was the first time that I had not been permanently marked. The slave master must have been an expert. A huge amount of debilitating pain but the skin hadn't been broked so I was not scarred.

"You have to learn that my clothes must always be perfect Ajax. What do you think would be an appropriate punishment for your dereliction of duty?"

He was being very imperious, but his manner made him appear very sexy and my wayward cock showed my arousal very quickly. It was very hard by the time Ptolomy had finished talking to me. The look on his face made me realise he had not seen my penis erect before. I didn't consider it to be huge, but it was certainly quite impressive. The master had enjoyed playing with it sometimes, but mostly he would just take me on his couch and fuck me quickly for mere satisfaction, he never made love to me. I think he found it easier to have the sex he wanted without all the complications of pregnancy and when he wanted to make love, he would take his wife.

So different to my life in Athens. My mentor showed me how joyous lovemaking between males could be, my father had picked well and I knew when my time came I would make my wife happy and mentor the son of a friend when I was older. At that moment , I had no idea what would happen to me. I supposed that if I was less comely I would be sent to one of the work gangs building the pyramid to house the next pharaoh to die and I would be worked to death.

Ptolemy took my cock in his hand and played with it for a few minutes making it even harder. Then he played with my balls as well. I loved it, he was being very gentle and when he looked into my eyes I could see the lust and realised that he was like me, a lover of sex and being a boy didn't detract from my attraction. It was some time before I realised that he was a boy lover and would never willingly bed a woman.

I was amazed. Instead of punishing me, he stroked my cheek with a hand before leaning to and kissed me on my lips. No man had ever done that before so I was quite surprised.

"Come Ajax, I have a different punishment for you," and he laughed, took my hand and lead me back to his rooms.

He made me lie down on his bed on my tummy and use my hands to spread my cheeks after he had got comfortable between my legs. He stroked my cheeks for a little while before moving his hands in close to my anus and spreading it even more. I felt something wet then, licking up and down my crack before stabbing at my hole. It felt incredible and I thought I was going to cum on the spot. My cock had never been so hard, and I had never been so excited. The action was called rimming and I had never experienced it before.

My mentor would play with my bottom to give me pleasure but he had never used his mouth on it, only on my cock and balls. I came up onto my knees and spread my legs even wider; I couldn't get enough of this action. He continued for some time, using his hands to play with me and stroke my cheeks as well.

When he had me almost ready to orgasm, he lubricated us and entered me quite gently, but all the way in one go. The spike of pain was not too bad because his father had used me so much that my sphincter was used to being stretched. He then fucked me the same as his father had, quite quickly and just to orgasm. When he had finished we rolled onto our backs and he told me he had enjoyed that. I thought he would enjoy it much more if he made love to me instead of just going for a quickie fuck.

"Ptolemy, if you will allow me, I will show you how to make love to a boy so that you can give yourself and your lover much more pleasure than you gave me."

"I took much pleasure from my action, how could you make it better for me?"

"Before I was captured my father placed me with a mentor who took much time showing me how to pleasure him and for him to pleasure me so that we both flew to Paradise as we made love. I can show you as well, either as the bottom boy or as the top if you would like me to put my penis inside you. I can also show you the great pleasure of being sucked to orgasm."

Ptolemy thought about this before replying.

"Do you not think I was a great lover then Ajax?"

"Oh yes, Master, but there is always more that we can learn together."

Of course I didn't mean that, apart from the rimming he really wasn't any better than his father. I think curiosity won because of his next comment.

"I should whip you for your insolence; being fucked by a master should give you untold joy."

"Yes Master, I'm sorry Master, this miserable slave knows that he is honored for being given your man juice."

That was just the right thing to say; he lay back on the bed and told me he would spare me the whip if I showed him how much better sex could be.

I started by kissing him softly on the lips to see how he reacted. I knew then that he was definitely a boy lover because masculine men didn't like being kissed on the lips by another of the same sex. I was more dominant then making the kisses very passionate, at the same time I started to caress his body, worrying his nipples as I caressed him. I moved down his body with my lips until I reached his nipples, which I nibbled until he came. I licked up his boy juice and immediately took his cock into my mouth to clean off the last of his emissions and bring him back to hardness. I swabbed his balls with my mouth as well while continuing to play with his cock.

I worked very hard then to make sure that he was continually just about ready to cum again but not letting him. I spread his legs and licked his perineum and tongue fucked him the same as he had done to me, but I kept pulling off when I felt he was about to cum again.

When he started to beg me to let him orgasm again, I straddled him and impaled myself on his cock, but even then I worked it very slowly so that I had two orgasms before I let him have one. His was incredibly severe so I fell forward to kiss him so that his squeals of delight were more subdued. I was satisfied that I had given him two orgasms that were far better than the one he had when he fucked me. I rolled sideways and let him remain in me until he was too soft then I rolled onto my back and waited.

"Oh Ajax, that was amazing. I have never enjoyed sex as much as that before. You must do that to me again and again." Then he laughed and pulled me into a cuddle.

Looking very serious he continued. "Would I get more pleasure from this if I let you fuck me instead of the other way round?"

"I don't know, Master, I could certainly give you an amazing experience but you may not like my cock inside you."

He sniggered and told me he was going to try it just to find out.

"You like it when I fuck you don't you Ajax?"

I laughed, "Oh yes, Master, always, but it is always better if I have been pampered first, the same as I did for you."

He could see the reasoning behind that having had two marvelous orgasms so he told me we would do that next time. I hoped we could then alternate being top and bottom. I did like to fuck and I hadn't done it since being captured. My mentor had taught me how to do it and I loved it. With Ptolemy it would be even better because he was my age and very beautiful.

When the big one happened I was very apprehensive. My cock was bigger than Ptolemy but I opened him up very carefully taking quite a long time to do so, alternating my tongue and my fingers. He was very beautiful and I so wanted to make him happy. I entered him very slowly, stopping after my glans had passed over his sphincter. I watched his eyes careful to make sure I kept the pain level low and sensitivity high. When I could see he was almost ready to orgasm, I pushed his thighs down harder spreading him wider and giving me deeper penetration and fucked him hard to orgasm, having mine at the same time.

For me it was ok, but because I was concentrating so hard on making my young master's orgasm so good it wasn't exceptional. The important thing was that Ptolemy had an incredible one that made him pass out for a few seconds, and then burst into tears of joy. He re-joined me slowly, realized how stupendous his orgasm was and nearly buried me in kisses.

"Oh, Ajax, I may never want sex any other way, that was the most stupendous experience of my life."

I was very pleased with myself and hoped that this experience would make my life much easier. In the event, my life changed so that I became a sex machine. Ptolemy told all his friends about the incredible slave who kept him sexually satisfied. I had to regularly satisfy some of them, usually fucking myself on their cocks. Only the boy lovers would let me fuck them and those I took to Paradise the same as I did Ptolemy. It was always one to one and usually only one other per day. Making love twice a day and looking after Ptolemy's clothes was all I had to do.

There was one problem that began to show and it was that I started to get fat. I quickly had to do something about that when it was mentioned, and not in a nice way. I then started a rigorous exercise regime that brought my body back in shape, and even improved it. I would run miles through the streets clad in just a breechcloth that showed my body to very good effect. I wore my slave anklet to show my status and was stopped frequently and asked who my master was. The result of that was the master being asked to sell me. The prices offered were much more than he had paid for me and he made it clear he was going to sell me to the highest bidder.

Ptolemy was most distraught and tried to dissuade his father from this action. The truth about Ptolemy and I came out then and the master was furious that I was loved not just used. I hadn't been to the punishment room for months so when the master took Ptolemy and myself there I was quite worried. The moment we were there we were made to strip naked, Ptolemy objected and the master slapped him very hard.

"You are a disgrace; a slave is for pleasure not for love. I am going to beat this illness from you."

Almost in shock at being chastised, Ptolemy stripped. He was too beautiful to look at that my cock betrayed me. The master looked at it and threatened that I wouldn't have it for very much longer. I was very frightened then. I knew that slaves that worked around the women of a house frequently lost their balls so that they could never impregnate the lady and make her pregnant, but to lose my cock as well filled me with the most awful terror.

"Strap my son to the punishment bench, Ajax and then fetch me the whip."

The whip, used properly could render unbelievable pain without breaking the skin. In the wrong hands it could also cripple the victim, splitting the skin and damaging the nerves. I had seen crippled slaves, paralyzed from the waist down with most awful scars on their buttocks and with their backs lacerated as well. I prayed that the master would not damage Ptolemy for I loved him so much.

The master was very efficient. He concentrated most of the strokes on his son's buttocks, straying to the back of the legs and the torso rarely, he delivered twenty-five, all of them with much power, but not breaking the skin, for which I was grateful. Ptolemy's screams made me want to run as they were so terrifying. Instead, the master told me to bring Ptolemy to him after he had recovered, and then he left. I had escaped unscathed, but I didn't expect that to last.

I spent nearly an hour applying soothing creams to the body of my young master and lover until he was comfortable.

"I love you so much Master, I pray the master will not part us."

Stood before the master we waited for his judgment.

"Unless you renounce this abomination and take a wife, Ptolemy, I will repeat that punishment every week. I will also remove Ajax manhood and send him to the building sites."

I was amazed, instead of complying with his father's wishes, he fell to his knees and told the truth.

"I love Ajax more than my life, Father, I will die if you hurt him or mutilate him."

It would have been so easy to comply with his father's wishes and still take me to his bed when he wanted me, but his love was too strong to accept that compromise. I was very flattered.

I had never seen the master so angry. I expected the most terrible retribution to be visited on both of us, but in my case death had to be the only outcome, either slowly on the buildings or in terrible agony in the punishment room. What happened to start with was the master storming out of the room almost puce with apoplexy. I immediately took Ptolemy in my arms and helped him back to his quarters. We didn't leave them for several days and his father never came near us. As time passed after the incident, the bruising and pain of the punishment gradually receded, but Ptolemy slowly deteriorated into a terrible depression. I became so worried that I went to the master on bended knees and pleaded with him to love Ptolemy again before he died of a broken heart.

The master was angry again, but I was the butt of his anger this time and he kicked me quite hard before telling me to go back to Ptolemy and look after him. I guess he needed to think and I hoped he would love his son enough to overcome his disgust at his sexuality.

The next action was two retainers coming to Ptolemy's quarters and removing me. Taken to the slave auction rooms I was beautified ready for sale. I noticed one of the young men in the crowd was one that I had made love to in Ptolemy's quarters. His father bid on me and became my new owner. Marcus was grinning as his father handed me over to him.

"I don't know why we had to have this one specifically Son, but he was very expensive so make sure you look after him."

When we arrived in his suite in another of the great houses, Ptolemy was waiting. He embraced his friend with very effusive thanks and kisses to go with it before bursting into tears and turning his attention to me.

"Oh, Ajax, I have missed you so much. I thought I would never see you again. My father will be very angry if he finds out, but I am virtually going to live here now so that the three of us can love each other."

I remembered then that Marcus was like Ptolemy, he was a boy lover and used to let me fuck him and the other way around as well. It looked as though I was going to be involved in many threesomes now. I thought that would be wonderful, I had never been spit roasted before but I could see that happening now and it thrilled me.

Ptolemy made love to me while Marcus watched the first time. When Ptolemy had gone home Marcus told me how things were going to work if I still wanted to make love to my true lover.

"Anything that happens when Ptolemy is not here is our secret. If you ever tell him I will let my father castrate you and send you to the mines. Do you understand?"

Of course I did, it was clear enough that I was going to see a side of Marcus I had not seen before.

"I worship the God of Phallus. You will be my sacrifice to him whenever I worship so we must prepare you. Come with me."

We went to a small private room that was lit by scented candles. Behind a small altar was a figure. The upper part was of a beautiful man, below the waist was animal. It had very hairy, but well muscled legs finishing in hoofed feet. In between his legs was a penis that would not have looked out of place on one of the chariot horses and it pointed upwards, with two very large balls hanging beneath. On an altar table just to the side was an exact copy of the cock and balls.

"Phallus has two cocks, only I may touch the one on his body, but when I pray he wants me to have his second cock embedded in my slave. So we are going to train you to take it."

I was in shock, the cock was enormous. I didn't think it was possible to even get the glans in my bottom, never mind the shaft. I also knew that this was all make-believe on the part of Marcus. There was no God of Phallus, it was just his kinky mind that had dreamed up this one.

"I do not expect you to take this today but I have a slave with a monster that will be used to train you ready for when I worship again. Come, let us go and see him."

We wandered down to the slave quarters, where up until now I hadn't been, to meet this man who was supposedly monstrously endowed. We walked out into the compound and Marcus called out the name, "Vega, to me."

A man turned his head and then walked towards us. He was black and quite slim, but between his legs hung a cock that reached a little way down his calf. It was the most enormous appendage I had ever seen. I'm quite sure that the stallions did not have longer ones than him. It was more than half as long as a man is tall and thicker than a man's forearm. I couldn't take my eyes from it. It wasn't an ugly cock and the ball sac must have been normal size because it was hidden behind the cock. I didn't believe it would get any longer when erect because there didn't appear to be anymore skin to stretch. Marcus must have read my mind.

"You will take a long time to get him an erection I think Ajax. It gets a little thicker and grows more, but only about the length of my thumb."

I didn't think that would matter, by the time he got to the last little bit I was sure I would be dead.

I looked round the compound and realized there were several adult slaves who were also incredibly well endowed, but none came close to Vega.

"Vega, bath, and then come to my rooms."

Turning to me he spoke again.

"We might as well start now, Ajax; I don't suppose we will be disturbed by Ptolemy."

There was to be no foreplay for this. I was positioned doggy fashion on a couch with my legs spread as wide as they would go.

"Vega, open him up as wide as you can with your fingers using plenty of lubrication. I will tell you when I think you should introduce your cock."

I was terrified. The fingers were quite normal, but I couldn't relax knowing what was to follow so the whole operation was quite painful. I felt his fist enter me and I screamed, but Marcus allowed him to carry on and I felt his arm slowly entering me.

"No further than the elbow, Vega, and then you can use your cock."

I felt his fist enter my intestines, another huge jolt of pain. Then it all became rather sensual. He fucked me with his arm for a little while until I started to relax and get an erection, then he pulled out and slid the first few inches of his cock into me. Again he was quite gentle and I was quite enjoying it until once again I felt my large intestine being stretched to take it and the pain returned.

I think I must have had about half of the monster inside me when the door opened and Ptolemy walked in. He took in the picture in a moment and just burst into tears.

"Oh, Marcus, what are you doing? You promised to look after Ajax for me, not abuse him."

Vega pulled out of me then and Ptolemy saw what had been inside me. He just gasped and stared at it not believing his eyes.

"Were you going to make Ajax take all of that?" The voice was so angry that Marcus cowered away from his friend. "You would have killed him if you had let the penetration finish. Are you mad?"

Marcus realized that Ptolemy was right when he took the time to think about it. Fortunately, Ptolemy was more worried about me, so he came to me and started to clean me gently, inspecting my anus for damage.

"If you had damaged him Marcus, I would have never forgiven you and devoted my life to obtaining revenge. Whatever possessed you to do this?"

Marcus was quite cowed by the anger in Ptolemy's voice and apologised, telling him about the fantasy of the God Phallus. They trooped down to see the figure of the God and when they came back they were laughing. I was more than a little upset at this, but the result was that Marcus never did anything that awful to me again, but I did have to be the bottom for some very big cocks while Marcus watched.

The best times though were the threesomes. I began to realise that I really did love boy/boy sex; being spit roasted by these two beautiful men was wonderful.

We had one foursome, which fascinated me because I watched another Greek slave called Demitri, who was bigger than me, fuck Marcus, who I realised was a true cock hound.

I was stood at the end of the couch with Ptolemy and we watched as Marcus lowered himself onto Demetri's impressive cock. I was massively hard and Ptolemy was obviously feeling wicked because he guided me over to the other two, lubricated my penis and made me enter Marcus as well. It was an incredible sensation fucking Marcus as he was fucking himself on Demitri's cock, which was sliding up and down my own. When we all came Demitri squealed with the power of his climax as did Marcus. As for me, my orgasm was so intense I actually passed out.

When we all recovered, Marcus told Ptolemy he was very wicked organising a double fucking, but that it was incredible and he was going to have that again sometime, probably with Ptolemy and me double fucking him. I almost passed out again just thinking about it.

My life now revolved around satisfying Ptolemy and Marcus with the occasional input of Demitri who would fuck either Marcus or me. It was marvelous; I had never been so contented as a slave.

This situation continued for many months and I suppose we all thought we had covered our actions very well, but Ptolemy's father became suspicious of his too frequent absences at the house of Marcus and sent a spy to find out what was going on. Because of that I ended up being dragged before the two fathers and the whole story was uncovered.

I was immediately removed from the house and incarcerated in a place for criminals. My wrists were chained together with the loop attached to a chain hanging from the roof. I don't know how long I hung there, days and nights rolled away and I lost count. I was given water occasionally but with no food, I weakened quickly. Lack of sleep and food took a dramatic toll until I lost consciousness. When I recovered I realized I was back in the house of Marcus's father. I was very weak, dehydrated and suffering from malnutrition. The slave that was looking after me told me what had happened.

"Ptolemy is dying, he told his father he didn't want to go on living without you, so the master was persuaded to have you brought from the prison and looked after."

I was surprised and asked how long I had been gone.

"Oh, almost six months."

I was dumbstruck, I had lost all sense of time and was delirious for so long of it that I had not realized the passing of half a year. I lifted the bedclothes to look at my body and was shocked. I was little more than a skeleton.

"I have been charged with looking after you and when you have been restored to your former beauty you are to be given to Ptolemy as a present."

I was almost overcome with happiness at that remark. After all the pain and misery I was going to be with my lover again and this time forever, hopefully.

Ptolemy was told of the arrangement but was not allowed to see me. I understood why. I am sure he would have died if he had seen the skeleton I had become. It took many months for me to regain the weight and size that I had been and I had to work very hard on my body to make sure I didn't become fat. At last the master considered I was fit to be seen and I was clothed in a beautiful tunic before being sent to Ptolemy's quarters. I was quite shocked, he looked nearly as bad as I had before being fed and looked after. I now had the most important job of my life, bringing my lover back to health and fitness.

It was a labor of love that took us another few months, but when we had achieved our aim I was able to look with love and admiration at the body of my lover. It was many years before anything changed in our life. I went everywhere with Ptolemy, always introduced as his companion, not his slave. Our lovemaking climbed to untold heights of satisfaction, always one to one.

It was when the Romans came that our lives started to change. The price of our capitulation was that Rome wanted many more slaves and Egypt would supply them. I was now in my thirties, no longer a great beauty, but known throughout the kingdom as a knowledgeable and powerful slave, having been brought up with Ptolemy as he climbed the social ladder.

The Roman commander decided I would go to Rome as the slave master. Ptolemy pleaded for me to remain with him, to no avail. On the day that I loaded the first batch of slaves onto the ship to go to Rome, with me accompanying them, Ptolemy came to kiss me goodbye and then, in front of me and the Roman in charge of this shipment, took out his knife and stabbed himself through the heart. His last words to me were, "I love you so much, I can't live without you," just as suddenly as he stabbed himself, he died in front of me.

I never recovered from the shock of the event and the death of my lover and eventually became a burden to my new masters so I was cast out to live as I may in a foreign land. After several years of wandering I eventually made my way back to my beloved Athens where I became a story teller of some note.

I am old now and live a reclusive life looking out from my small home onto the city that I love, and dreaming of how it could have been if I had Ptolemy with me.

~~The End~~

Here is a sample from another story you may enjoy:

Prisoner
of
His Heart

Hot Gay Romance
Chris Johns

Might as well do as I'm asked; I need a shower anyway, was the thought that ran through Matt's head as he sniffed his armpits.

Fifteen minutes later Alexander was back.

"Come with me," was all he said.

"But I have no clothes."

"You won't need them."

"But—"

"No buts, boy; do as you are told and come with me."

Feeling extremely embarrassed, Matt did as he was told. He had to find out what was going on, and the only way he could think to do that was to talk to the man by the pool.

Matt was nineteen and guessed the man on the sun bed to be about ten years older. As he approached, keeping a little behind Alexander, Matt noted the man, as he stood up, was probably an inch or two taller than him, well put together, without being over muscled. He couldn't see the eyes, which were covered with a pair of designer sun glasses, but noted the mid brown hair and the aquiline features, the golden tan with a dusting of hair on the chest, and, finally, the very pronounced bulge in his Speedos. He wasn't quite sure why his brain noted that fact particularly; men had never held his interest; women hadn't either, but he thought that being spaced out on drugs so often had put his sexual desires to sleep.

He stopped in front of the man and started to speak, but the man put a finger to his lips and stood in front of him.

"Listen, Matt, and learn. You will speak when spoken to, and you will obey every order given to you by me or my staff."

Matt interrupted, "Who the fuck are you?"

It was definitely the wrong thing to say. The man nodded, and before Matt could react, Alexander had him bent over a poolside table and delivered ten very hard slaps with his hand to Matt's bare arse.

Alexander was probably about six feet six inches tall, and around 225 pounds of what looked like solid muscle. A spanking from those hands was not something to want twice. Matt was howling when he was again stood facing the man, tears streaming down his face.

"As I was saying, you will call me Master at all times, and Alexander you will address as Sir. If you wish to speak, other than to answer a question, you will ask, 'Permission to speak, Master, or Sir', and wait to be given permission before continuing. If you utter any more profanities, you will be punished. Do you understand those instructions?"

Matt felt resentful, and made his second mistake.

"Yes," he mumbled.

Alexander was on him in a flash, delivering another very hard swat to his already very red ass. Matt yelped and jumped forward, almost knocking the Master over.

"Yes, what, Matt?" The man barked out.

"Yes, Master," was the now much more precise reply.

"Good. Now then, we are going to start cleaning you up before trying to turn you back into a civilised human being, inside as well. When I am finished, you will go with Alex. All of those disgusting bits of metal on you will be removed, and you will be given a respectable haircut. Then you can rejoin me for lunch. Tomorrow, you will be taken to a hospital for plastic surgery to restore your ear lobes to their proper shape. The following day, you will undergo laser treatment to remove all those tattoos, and then we will be left with a human being on the outside, instead of some painted and pierced animal. We will then spend however long we have to, training you to return to society as a useful and civilized person. Do you understand?"

Matt was fuming! "You can't do that! Let me go! You have no right to do this!" He was almost beside himself with anger, but not for long. Alexander was on him again and delivered another ten very hard slaps to a pair of cheeks already showing bruising from the first ten. Stood in front of the Master again, Matt was informed that there would be no more bare hand spankings.

"If you need chastising again, Matt, it will be with a cane. Do you understand?"

Through his sobs, Matt replied with a shaking voice, "Yes, Master."

To purchase the book, look for **More Than A Friend**.

From the Author

If you enjoyed any of my books then please share the love and click like on my books in Amazon.

If you write me a review and send me an email I will send you a free book, or many.
(Just know that these emails are filtered by my publisher.)

Good news is always welcome.

One Last Thing, For Kindle Readers...

When you turn the page, Kindle will give you the opportunity to rate this book and share your thoughts on Facebook and Twitter. If you enjoyed my writings, would you please take a few seconds to let your friends know about it? Because... when they enjoy they will be grateful to you and so will I.

Thank You!

Dexter Chase
dexter_chase@awesomeauthors.org

www.ingramcontent.com/pod-product-compliance
Lightning Source LLC
Chambersburg PA
CBHW071355130626
46556CB00005B/2195